A Short History of
the Island of Butterflies

A Short History
of the
Island of
Butterflies

POEMS BY

Nicholas
Christopher

VIKING

VIKING
Viking Penguin Inc., 40 West 23rd Street, New York, New York 10010, U.S.A.
Penguin Books Ltd, Harmondsworth, Middlesex, England
Penguin Books Australia Ltd, Ringwood, Victoria, Australia
Penguin Books Canada Limited, 2801 John Street, Markham, Ontario, Canada L3R 1B4
Penguin Books (N.Z.) Ltd, 182–190 Wairau Road, Auckland 10, New Zealand

First published in 1986 by Viking Penguin Inc. in simultaneous hardcover and paperback editions
Published simultaneously in Canada

"The Public Gardens," "Winter Night," "Evening," "Leaving Town," "The House Where Lord
Rochester Died," "Cardiac Arrest," "Losing Altitude," and "Musical Chairs" originally appeared
in *The New Yorker*; "Lineage," "Night of the Quarter-Moon in August," and "The Partisan" in
Grand Street; "Mars and Venus," "Voyage," "Mountain and Valley," "Icarus," "Reflections on a
Bowl of Kumquats, 1936," "Blizzard," and "Verona, 1973" in *The Nation*; "Sunday, Looking
Westward" in *The Paris Review*; "The City of Love" in *Fiction International 14*; "Orange Light" and
"Quatrains for Sunlight" in *Shenandoah*; "Waiting for the Revolution" and "The Other Woman" in
River Styx; "Blondes and Brunettes" in *Harvard Magazine* and "Jeoffry the Cat" and "Blood Test"
in *Medical Heritage*.

Acknowledgment is made for permission to reprint the following copyrighted material: Excerpt
from *The Magician's Garden and Other Stories* by Geza Csath, translated by Jascha Kessler and
Charlotte Rogers. © 1980, Columbia University Press. By permission.

Excerpt from *Remembrance of Things Past*, Volume Two, by Marcel Proust, translated by C. K. Scott
Moncrieff and Terence Kilmartin. Translation copyright © 1981 by Random House, Inc., and
Chatto & Windus. Reprinted by permission of the publisher.

LIBRARY OF CONGRESS CATALOGING IN PUBLICATION DATA
Christopher, Nicholas.
A short history of the island of butterflies.
I. Title.
PS3553.H754S56   1986   811'.54   85-40573
ISBN 0-670-80899-7

Printed in the United States of America by
R. R. Donnelley & Sons Company, Harrisonburg, Virginia
Set in Palatino

For my mother and father

I would like to thank:

Howard Moss, whom I can never thank enough for his great faith and generosity;

Anthony Hecht, who by example and encouragement helped make the crooked road that much straighter;

and for their generous assistance: my wife, Constance Christopher, Paul and Allison Vlachos, John Paul Itta, and Robert Cullen.

We would wonder, to see a Man, who in a wood,
were left to his liberty to fell what trees he would,
take only the crooked, and leave the straytest
trees; but that man hath perchance a ship to build,
and not a house . . .

—JOHN DONNE, *Sermons*

CONTENTS

The use of this symbol (~) at the bottom of the page indicates a stanza break.

I

THE PUBLIC GARDENS

Someone might mistake the shadows
of the loners for sleeping animals,
the darting light for a bird of prey.

The palms shiver reflections
across the fountain, and the goldfish
glide through channels of algae.

On wet evenings they jump for
cigarettes or gum; in a drought
they surface belly-up, full of death.

Ancient architects centered this city
around the Public Gardens—the dark
hub to a wheel of radiating streets.

They run fast and straight for miles,
but at the city limits
they go black, they empty.

Around the fountain the weeping willows,
filled with nightingales, glint
like cages in the moonlight.

Under the cones of lampposts,
the statues of nymphs and satyrs
survey the blue trees

where the solitary lovers
and the lost children—
all those who have paid dearly

for their corner of the night—
curl into the shadows
like cats and count the stars.

~

A single guard is asleep at the gate,
dreaming of the treetops like wavelets
rippling under alpine winds,

and of the city's dead
in garish dress, waving to the statues
from their funeral trains,

and of the river beyond the suburbs
where the boulevards end,
where the air is black and rainy

and the foliage opens like a curtain
onto millions of bright flowers.

CARDIAC ARREST

This is the time when the gods come
for your heart.
Down the long blue corridors,
past one door, then another,
a last dark turn and then—
light. Simplicity of motion,
of gestures, in a gallery
of white shadows.
And you dream without sleeping:
of miners who scrape coal
from the earth like roe from a fish;
of the monks in hell
with the lead-lined cloaks;
of obsidian eels at a hundred fathoms
who have witnessed the birth of whales;
of the hands against a golden light
which bathed and combed you
and turned you in your sleep.
You are flat on the sidewalk
of a busy city street
and a crowd has gathered to watch
the policeman loosen your collar.
High, high in the sunlight
a construction crane raises a man
in a cage—a deus ex machina
swaying against the clouds.
Truly, the man could be a god,
rising even higher now, escaping
with your heartbeat in the palm of his hand.

A Short History of
the Island of Butterflies

The courtyard fills with them at dead of noon,
orange and yellow clouds under the cloudless sky,
clustering in the thick eucalyptus,
alighting on the loud hibiscus,
forever shaping and coloring the tropical
stillness in the seasons when the wind tails off.
The schoolgirls dream chrysalis-dreams
as the butterflies cover their windows
like shrouds—black shadows flapping up
from the cistern's depths—
and across the bay, on Antíparos,
the pirates' skeletons scrawl
graffiti in the marble quarries,
updating their messages from the beyond,
where the mania for conquest and plunder
led them one winter's dusk,
strung up by a band of widows
and left blindfolded for the crows—
agents of treachery, hated by the old gods.
Here the crows are white, often mistaken
for gulls, and they nest in the stunted
mountain pines, in a grim exile.
Those women, suppliants to St. Mark,
were not always so fierce,
but that Christmas their husbands
were butchered after the sultan dreamt
of long-haired men with scythes
ambushing him in a lemon grove;
of all his colonies, Paros
was famous for its lemons,
so the Turks beheaded fifty men
on a barge in the harbor
and tossed their bodies to the fish.
And in the men's eyes,
and in the pirates' eyes,
under their blindfolds,

danced thousands of silver butterflies.
From then on, the widows dressed
in their husbands' clothes, and wore
kerchiefs folded over like butterfly wings
and earrings fashioned of bees dipped in amber,
and, later, with drawn scimitars,
they helped to rout the sultan's fleet,
thus fulfilling his nightmare.
Some of them lived into their eighties
and nineties, long enough
to see the young English poet arrive
with his entourage of rogues and monkeys,
he in Albanian dress, a pashá,
outfitted with white turban and wolfskin cape
as he sailed into that same harbor
under a brilliant sun
and declared himself in Paradise.
He behaved well at first,
attended mass and distributed alms,
but they best remember him
for the dueling pistols he demonstrated
at the monastery in Márpissa,
shooting a cigar from a novice's teeth,
and for swimming the channel at Náoussa by starlight,
and for the night he was rowed, on his horse,
out to Drionísi, gray and smoky islet,
where he cantered till dawn, singing in Italian.
The next day (as he'd done at Sounion and Delphi—
it was a familiar routine)
he chiseled his name onto a pillar
and sailed for Rhodes,
leaving his pistols for the holy abbot;
and on their ivory handles, embossed in gold,
shone a pair of Monarch butterflies.
Other visitors have left their calling-cards:
the Venetians their balconies and chapels,
the Romans their paving stones,
the French their Haitian parakeets,
the Russians their silver cannon . . .
They plundered too, like the pirates,
mostly boatloads of marble—

even the Parthenon blocked in
Parian white, finer than Carrara—
and for just as long, long before Byron
(since Archílochos penned the first ode in Léfkes),
the poets have come for their own sort of booty,
for music so palpable it honeys the air,
chords of light and shadow humming
from the white mazes of the towns
and the silver grids of the olive groves.
Today the flying fish precede my ship to Santorini,
and in our wake the gulls wheel as one—
no, they are crows, white and treacherous
and most fortunate: for they will return
to the island of the sweet winds,
where the butterflies' wings are etched
with a tiny script, with volumes of history
no one will read, and bright maps
that fold at midnight into memories.

EVENING

An old man crosses the wet lawn
at dusk as the swallows dip
between the rows of elms.
He passes through the gate in the hedge,
his boots crowfooted with cut grass,
and his white coat catches the gleam
from an upstairs lamp
as he stops to light a cigar,
which then, like a June bug
on fire, precedes him
through the thistles and brush,
over the salt grass like mermaids' hair
and the tiny highways of the fast crabs,
down to the ragged field by the sea.

The dolphins zigzag, and the seafloor
mirrors up its silver darkness,
and the roses bloom in the clouds
escaping the continent—
but what is it that rivets him
and stirs him to laughter
on that bluff where the breakers'
music, like shrouds of gravel covering
and uncovering the dead, reduces younger
men to taut humility or silence?
An hour passes, and the gulls,
custodians of that slow borderline,
follow him back as far as the gate,
and by then the swallows are perched
and the black owls alert
and the big house ablaze with lights
as the ember of his cigar floats across
the dark lawn, and with a startling cry,
amplified by the quick wind,
the children hiding behind the cold elms
rush out to greet him.

LINEAGE

Here's a photograph taken in Manhattan in 1891.
From a rooftop looking south
on the first day of summer.
A man with a cane is smoking in a doorway,
watching a woman alight from a carriage.
A dog is crouching at his heels.
The flags are at half-mast.
In the distance, in Union Square, construction is underway
on another office building,
and some falling bricks just scattered the pigeons.
It was the year before my grandfather was born.
The clock on the bank reads 9:30.
Across from the bank is a theater.
On the sidewalk a vendor is examining a peach
and a policeman is gazing at the sky.
Two boys are rolling a hoop under the marquee.
All of them are dead now.

That same day my great-grandmother was on her honeymoon.
Sitting by the window of the bridal suite
in an Athens hotel,
staring out across the night at the fiery bougainvillea
that rings the Royal Gardens.
Her husband is asleep on the couch
under a thick blue shadow.
She has wrapped his jacket around her shoulders.
She is seventeen years old.
Eight months later she will die in childbirth,
but her son—my grandfather—will survive.
Eventually, he will emigrate and settle in Manhattan.
My father and I will be born there,
and I will write this poem there on a summer day,
on another rooftop.

In the photograph there is also a girl in a hotel window.
She is looking directly at the photographer, through the sunlight.

She is very pale, her eyes are wide,
and she resembles my future wife.
The clock on the bank still reads 9:30,
but it appears some in the crowd have moved:
the vendor has pocketed the peach
and the man with the dog is crossing the street
and the boys' hoop is lying in the gutter.
The girl in the window has changed, too.
Her face has darkened and her gaze is averted—
as if someone has called to her from across the room.
Across the years.

The Customs Inspector

I love to sail forbidden seas, and land on barbarous coasts.
    —HERMAN MELVILLE, *Moby-Dick*

Once I had written my masterpiece
and settled all debts fathoms deep
and scratched up new ones here, on the dusty streets
of Manhatto, children to feed and a wife half-mad,
I might have found worse callings than this:
sifting through the world's cargoes,
the dank holds of the schooners, and the ladies'
portmanteaux where the coiled silks might conceal
Persian trinkets or emeralds or dangerous flowers.
I walk every day from Chelsea to the Battery
in my black coat and boots, and I lunch alone
on the docks, avoiding fish and sea flesh,
watching the brigs come and go,
serene and white in the obscure light.
I see the riggers in their red caps, straining,
and the foretopman staring back to port,
and the circling gulls that follow them out so far
and then return against the trailing wind.
My youth was exhausted in flying from these shores;
like a Bedouin, I knew the blue desert before I knew a woman.
But that's over now. At home we have a fine lime tree
in the garden, and when the sun works its way around
the steeples, I like to sit flooded in the soft light
that sets the birds darting through the shadows.
They say I've come off easy—
old friends, the relatives, my son who shot himself—
that I was not fit for what I stumbled on,
the Pandora's boxes I mistook for men's souls.
But I put it to you that none of the others
had the spine to go where I went, to dream
the screaming bird of prey nailed to the sinking mast,
the whirlpool flung from the eye of the dying whale,
and the white wall that men hit against in the blinding
darkness when they take the one, last step that matters.

I was there, after the deluge, in the milky haze,
watching a bonfire of shipwrecks on the seafloor,
my fingers gripping a slippery plank
and the sky broken in two.
In the mornings, when I dress, my wife watches from the shadows;
she says my sleep clatters with unfamiliar voices;
she says she hears a roaring in her ears;
she says there is no mercy in my silence.
I believe her.

QUATRAINS FOR SUNLIGHT

There is no past or future,
no time for calculations,
just the light gliding over brick
and the heat seeping through the trees.

Central Park is deserted, dusty,
some bums and chess players, and a girl
sunning the box of tomato plants
she's lugged down from her apartment.

Cyclists are outracing trucks and buses,
and truants, smoking cigarettes like
Jean Gabin (whom they have never heard of),
are dealing ganja by Longfellow's statue.

Though sometimes I walk this city
swimming the crosscurrents of my desires,
often I feel I've wandered onto some enormous
film lot, a 3-D extravaganza made in Japan.

All the windows have their stories,
layered like the long years,
and the faces, from deadbeat to Raphael blonde,
are works-in-progress, by turns comic and tragic.

The down-at-heels accountant, unhappy lawyer,
oversexed doctor—every stereotype plods
these sidewalks exactly as one imagines them,
recreated out of fiction—but with quirks, surprises.

And yet, even the oddballs, the hybrids,
can be anticipated, and assimilated:
the janitor who builds music boxes,
the mailman who writes pornographic verse . . .

~

Nothing here can really be called "eccentric"—
outside the circle—for by Augustine's
definition, this city is a circle, magnetic ring
to which every odd & end on the continent flies.

From a rooftop, everything changes.
The royal blue sky at my fingertips,
I could be in Atlantis, plunging to sea-bottom
atop a mass of towers and rubble.

Or, scanning from east to west,
river to river, the great gray blur
of streets and crowds might be the microscopic
grain on a meteor hurtling through oblivion.

Or what I think I see already may have disappeared,
transposed—like Rome's power—to Byzantium,
and the light on this summer morning no more
than a filter for my misperceptions, a screen.

Coffee black, ham & eggs, wheat toast,
two *petit coronas*, notebook and pen,
hot shower cold shower close shave: I am
most occupied in maintaining habits, and silence.

Expanding my fantasies or limiting my movements,
I take pleasure in keeping to myself,
at the center of a great hubbub, within the human
bull's-eye that awaits illumination's arrow.

But with or without me, the metropolis hums on,
labyrinth upon labyrinth of stock players—
tyrants, queens, heroes, and jesters—
all secure in their certain expendability.

For however clouded the purpose, or soiled
the hours lost to putting bread on the table,
everyone must labor with mind detached
and feet in the mud, grounded by necessity.

So that only the supernal, jewel-like yet expansive,
like the vast planes and spirals within

a sapphire, and the azure plains in my heart,
can bring me to life amid the clatter.

If I walk outside my cell and my self,
even in such a stark maze as this,
where the mad mount pulpits and the timid
leap from bridges—even here I may find peace.

Or at least a religion of streets, inspired one unto
the other, howling canyons and snaking tunnels,
flesh and machinery interbred at high speed,
and sunlight, awakened to cast each moment in gold.

WINTER NIGHT

Burning torches line the floor of the sea.
Women in white hurry along the beach,
into the mist, with a pack of dogs.
It is past midnight.
Airplanes, every few minutes, fly out from the land,
over the bluffs where the stripped trees
line up like crosses in a military graveyard.
A lighthouse beams its small yellow moon onto the breakers,
and the big moon hangs behind the scudding clouds.
The women pause at the jetty and loosen their hair.
The dogs leap through the surf with muffled cries
and run in circles around the dim figures
that have appeared in the shallows:
men with smoky faces and limbs,
robed in sheets of blue light.
The women stare past them, mesmerized by the torches.
The airplanes are growing louder and more frequent.
It is cold and the gray sand has slicked itself into glass.
The women skate back up the beach against the whistling wind,
and the dogs dive through the black curtain where the water deepens,
and the men disappear in a burst of spray.
The torches float up to the surface, like the reflections of stars.
On the bluffs, the trees still resemble crosses in a graveyard.
It is a graveyard.
Across the sea the war has ended.
Those were the airplanes gone to fetch the wounded.
Those were the dead, watching the waves come in.

THE PARTISAN

I was eating black olives in the sun
when the bullets whistled through my heart
and I heard children singing.
I glimpsed soldiers behind the rocks,
but my last impression was of my wife,
whose hair was blond as the field
flying away from under me.
Even as a student I had prepared myself
for that day, the hour I would be led
to a stained wall or makeshift gallows,
blindfolded with set jaw and clenched fists;
I never imagined I might be ambushed
over my lunch, years after my last skirmish,
temples graying and old wounds blued into scars;
I had not even a delusion of my own martyrdom.
No followers, no weapon in my belt:
how they found me, why they were still pursuing,
and what price lay on my head, I'll never know.
I hadn't read a newspaper in years.
Nor spoken to a single soul.
I remembered the streets of the capital,
not as a maze of police and barricades,
but with nostalgia, with a boy's memory
of carnivals and parades, of my father
at the edge of a crowd smoking his white pipe.
In hiding, I devoured books of medicine and astronomy,
Pliny and Galen, Kepler and Galilei.
For a while, I considered going abroad.
Too late.
They buried me on the spot, in my boots and hat,
carpeting the grave with pine needles and stones,
blending them carefully into the texture of the hillside.
As if nothing had happened.
Rifling my pockets, closing my eyes,
they overlooked but one detail:
my mouth which never opened again,

which clamped shut with an olive pit under the tongue;
even now, I am waiting for the tree that will one day
burst forth, casting its shadow in my image—
plunging them into darkness.

Leaving Town

The trumpeter in the mariachi band
dreamt again of a landlocked swan.

Of the blue desert
under a moon filled with seawater.

The drummer overslept as usual
and the band left him behind.

They were staying in the hotel
with the broken fountain.

Last night the drummer posed for pictures
with the girls at the Triangle Club.

This was between the band's two sets
at the Café Barracuda, next door.

The trumpeter also missed the train
this morning, but for personal reasons.

He had glimpsed a woman he used to know
(her hair dyed black) getting off an elevator.

The two musicians ate lunch
downtown, at a chop-suey joint.

In the distance the mountains
shimmered behind the desert wind.

The drummer recounted his evening's adventures,
but the trumpeter wasn't listening.

He was thinking back on old times
with the woman—another city, another life.

~

A July afternoon of flatbed trucks
rushing by with slabs of ice.

And crazy sirens. And a dozen people
dead of heat exhaustion. And endless quarrels.

All the same quarrel, about a woman
who had lied to both of them and run away.

That night they had gone to the park
and watched the river through the elms.

Separately, they counted the sapphires
the moonlight was laying on the far bank.

The drummer, weary of talking, bought some cigars
and asked the waiter where he could score opium.

Then he wired ahead to the band in the next town
and reserved two seats on the train.

The trumpeter called the hotel
and left a message for the woman.

Later, at the station, he told
the drummer he was quitting the band.

The drummer wished him luck
and borrowed ten dollars.

The trumpeter bought a bouquet of roses
and returned to the hotel.

At the desk they told him the woman had received
his message, and left town on the afternoon train.

REFLECTIONS ON A BOWL OF KUMQUATS, 1936

The exemplar of the calculating squint
and the surreptitious kick to the shin,
of the fight to the finish, no holds barred;
the juggler with billiard balls and oranges,
interchangeable in a blur—
like Life&Death at the heart of the farce:
bite into the wrong thing in the dark and watch
the teeth fly like sparks, everybody laughing . . .
Sly, slyer than cats and lady druggists,
more familiar than house dicks with the bright evil
gritted into the fabric of things, of "everyday life,"
so many places to avoid, and dreams,
the man in the four-way mirror outflanking his insomnia,
pockets stuffed with bankbooks,
closely shaven even at two a.m.
Let double-talk patch the fearsome wind,
a crazyquilt of insults and anxious asides,
only the children, who threatened him, equipped
to read the barometer of that face,
the short degrees between spite and rage,
degrees of applause and betrayal,
of the dinginess of rooms, of the lost years
notched with a penknife on his traveling trunk.
Now see the sun setting behind the palms,
see the weedless lawn and the Florentine fountain,
see the clay court steaming through the vines,
see Hollywood to the north dirty and pink;
tailored in white with rakish Panama, chewed corona,
the nimble fat man sips gin from a halved tennis ball,
shows the vicious backhand patented for laughs, for winning.
Only the stray dogs at the gate can appreciate that.
Never give a sucker an even break.

LOSING ALTITUDE

Plummeting past the birds,
millions of them flapping by,
the orange cloudbank a warren of ghosts,
of ghostly chatter still audible
above the whine of our twin engines,
our racing four-chambered hearts.

Is this the way to Xanadu—
slicing through the earth in seconds
to emerge upside down in China?
Or, rather, the route Elijah took,
fooling us with mirrors
as he fell to heaven?

There is no way of knowing anything.
And no one here to soothe us.
The only consolation is Zeno's:
each of our few remaining seconds
halved infinitely until we are left
with sunlight, sky, and eternity.

The altimeter keeps the time,
running down to zero o'clock
when the merciful angels
will ring their golden bells
and the flamethrower angels
douse us with immortality.

In these last miles the air
thickens to blue mist
riddled with flickering windows
in which impassive faces ebb and flow,
peering past their own shadows,
all of them vaguely familiar . . .

~

A lifetime of faces, from cities
we walked, stations and terminals,
all the journeys that led us here—
without parachutes or prayers—
where the white sea rushes up
at breakneck speed to welcome us.

Passing Through the Torrid Zone

The lonely summer nights empty into one another.
Speedboats cast blue shadows along the breakwater.
Enormous clouds creep over the horizon
showering spices into the lazy waves,
and old men bait their lines with mirrors
and fish from the moldy piers.
Mist roils up the mountainside,
bathing the town in green vapors
and cooling into rain at dawn.
The hotels are empty, paint peeling
in wet strips like mango flesh,
snails trailing cobalt on the tiles,
and spiders nesting in the keyholes.
Visitors dream about the volcano
(dormant for ninety years)
and the rumors of orgiastic cults,
shipwrecked mariners and youthful witches
who roam the interior.
Dining alone, on rock crabs and melon,
I find a certain majesty in the jagged
layout of this town, the haphazard architecture:
crosshatchings of bamboo and ebony,
ramshackle porches and florid byways,
stairwells thick with moss
and alleys paved with fishbones and coral,
and a yacht club—
that gaudy colonial throwback—
which looks like a pagoda designed on mescaline:
flying buttresses and Buddhist friezes
and a terra-cotta roof with silver gutters.
A littered promenade connects it to the ruins
of the governor's mansion,
its seawall lined with ornate benches
where the gentry lounged on Sundays
to watch sailboats circle the bay.
Now parakeets sip from craters

on the tennis court, the fountain
is tunneled through with mice,
and cats are mating in the starlit gazebo.
Even the raw colors of the harbor—
splashing yellow, phosphorus orange,
and creamy oyster pink—
suggest the residue of an abandoned empire,
brilliant patches flung back by
receding tides, spreading outward
to the jungle's perimeters.
It's a place where discarded vices
return, like the cigarettes
I am smoking again with my coffee,
and the straight rum I order at lunch,
and the string of gin rickeys that follow dinner,
guiding me unsteadily into the glazed
morning hours at the zinc bar
with its incense and disco music,
where the bargirls all want to go
to America—like everyone else—
in their T-shirts and hot pants and heels,
their small soprano voices husky
around the edges and their purple
fingernails bitten down.
Are these the descendants of those
butter-skinned mermaids who swam out
to greet Cook and Drake,
who could spearfish and pearl-dive
better than any man, white or brown?
They have something to give me,
they insist, but I've stopped here,
in transit between continents,
not in order to give or take anything,
but to observe, to be on the outside
looking in—a phantom;
after many such expeditions
over the years, I should know better,
that this observer's role never works out,
and if not jail or the infirmary
or a hopeless one-night stand,
something will develop,

the phantom will flesh out,
and the flesh, true to its maxim, will be frail.
But not tonight, for I am quite alone
with my frailty and my flashlight,
on the road into the mountains,
at the last dusty curve
from which I can still see the town,
a bedraggled scrap of quilt
tossed alongside the silver bay,
lit on a long angle from seaward
by the orchid moon,
nestled below the steaming volcano,
in the path of every stray hurricane and squall;
like the human heart, I tell myself,
which in a matter of seconds can jump
from heat to cold, radiance to gloom,
always threatened with extinction,
but, somehow, with its tenuous pale threads,
putting down roots, waiting to be forgotten,
or engulfed by pleasure—
as if such luxuries were still possible in this world.

THE CITY OF LOVE

Another persuasive argument for the erotic
memory as universal truth.

Why Byron's Venice (1819) was
the Hollywood of its day.

The churning, brackish canal
of pleasure craft,

cathedrals for trysting,
bordellos for prayer,

poets jamming the Bridge of Sighs
and widows at vespers keening.

The myriad courtyards radiate scarlet
oaks, and weary virgins,

and ladies bleached in mist
on splendid balconies

working to unriddle desires
overripened as fruit, unyielding

as the virgins, whom candlelight unpetals,
like roses, to buds of steel.

There are thorns tipped for paradise
and fronds fired for hell,

cities bypassed by dreams
yet populated with dreamers,

stairways of sinners between
setting sun and rising moon.

~

The vaporetto lit like a cake
cuts the holiday night,

swirl of revelers, clowns, police,
and the bride as figurine

abandoned on the quay, laced in rain,
cold and sweet with the promise

of fantasy, of ideals,
of her betrothed, the young sailor,

who dreamt himself as fish, to music,
and swam away to sea.

THE MILKY WAY FROM BRENDA'S LAWN

The Lone Ranger used to ride his horse
Silver down that glittering road.
Pythagoras mapped it out for him.
Outlaws, behind boulders, fired black
bullets into the night, hoping for
their small share of notoriety,
and made the mistake of their lives.
A thirst for evil (with its adrenal kick)
lured them to shallow graves
on a distant moon—silver bullets,
like stars, lodged in their hearts.

Brenda is singing to the silver owls
in the apple orchard, waiting for
them to swoop up across the sky.
She's been watching the luxury liners
sail in from deep space along
their gulfstream of crushed diamonds.
I tell her that the Milky Way is too many
stars to count, more than all the people
who have ever lived or died,
and that none of us can expect more
than a single star to shine truly
in our eyes, our hearts, on the tip
of our tongues, before we're gone.

MUSICAL CHAIRS

You start with the dancing girls,
move on from there.

Bouquets, incense, endless games
of musical chairs in the clouds.

After some years, your tread loses
its spring, your hand its sweep,

the words that leapt in persuasion
barely float on the narrowing stream.

It is at this point the great diarists err:
turning to religion, or drugs.

Turning, with brackish concurrence,
to a jaded sea, the salt and sleet

that whirls out memories.
And the vapors of regret,

and sorrow in the charting of tides,
and the open wound marbled and elegized—

like all deep-sea monuments,
designed to misguide the young,

to sustain the supremacy
of that old port of call.

Where the gamesters play for hearts
with a shaved deck.

Where the music accelerates
and the chairs disappear.

You start with the dancing girls.
They never let you go.

II

SUNDAY, LOOKING WESTWARD

1.

A wall of fire steals across the prairie
and the string quartet in the downstairs parlor
breaks off suddenly when a blizzard of light invades our sleep,
our overlapping dreams which we dismiss knowingly, sweetly,
as the mirror of our passing lives, the music on the other side
of ourselves that never breaks off—or so we pray
on such mornings as these, Sunday amid the alfalfa,
two hills' distance from the green river and its fertile banks,
its hot mud of baptism and forgetting and slow birth.
In these high white rooms the gold dust of wheat and maize
hangs passively behind sunlit curtains, and the conversation
of the barefoot girls wafts up to us from the road,
the easy bells of their voices that will ring in our ears
long after they are gone and talked past their passionate and idle
adventures of the night, the quicker passion of innocence,
which for us has become so many murky dreams and quartets
and preoccupations (like baggage) hastily packed and easily lost.
As if in coming here, to these spaces, open and unbounded,
we sought to relinquish the harsher aspects of our solitude,
the granite corridors and violent crowd scenes from other people's
tragedies, and the murderous clowns in our own comedy.
Here it's the flatness drives young men to despair,
and while we seek only long vistas and plenitude of light,
perhaps their—this other—despair will lead us
to the brink of something fruitful and bright, to the river's
edge in the packed early light of goshawks and crows,
the river of pain and plenty, of landlocked lovers
and the sinful downstream melodies that too seldom distract them.
For the interloper, especially, understands this fixation
on the hazy passionless fields unbounded more clearly
than he views his own landscape of solitude (and music).

2.

There is that golden, sexless smell of baked bread
climbing the side of the house, surviving the hot scents

of the roses and the vaporous tangle of honeysuckle,
curling up through bushes and vines crisscrossed
by the murmuring bees—the smell of white
bread glazed with butter cooling on a windowsill.
The horses left to pasture ramble from fence to fence
and a black cat streaks through the red flowerbeds
and someone in the parlor mentions yesterday's funeral
and tomorrow's dance an instant before the interrupted quartet
resumes its shiver and throb of heartstrings and bass,
winding a false promise of rain through the warm house.
And we wonder what ratio of fear and desire
we have brought to this place under the rollicking clouds—
we the privileged visitors transported from the labyrinth
with such apparent ease, content for the moment
to whirl safflower honey onto our heated bread,
to take our pick of the golden horses
and snatch up a bouquet of damp carnations
before setting out across the river for yet another dance.
And is this so much peace and contentment
as the indulgence of the dream that a place not our own
(like certain music, forever on the other side of ourselves)
is by definition that much more paradisal or infernal?
When we are very young, it is the exotic brings this out;
but as we drift on, the exotic grows tiresome and velvet-worn
and places like these, with their pollen clouds and pastel
rains and windy river basins, begin to fuel
our passage away from ourselves.

    3.

Dusk, soft and pervasive, pearls a haze over the river.
That solitary horse in the far field is always the last to come in,
his black mane in the failing sun lit up red as iron,
as he rears slowly, pacifically, before the wind sweeps
over him cold and dry.
That faint touch of blue, of ice, in the summer night
is like a child's first comprehension of death.
And for the children here, familiar with the butcher's block
and the barnyard cycles,
the deaths of men, stripped of pomp and excess,
may bite but rarely poison.

All this uncluttered sky keeps death simple—
like a wolf allowed so many chickens before he is hunted down.
The wolves must come and go whether we loathe
or welcome them, or stalk them through the high grass,
become wolves ourselves, rock-bellied and white-eyed.
Now that lone horse, nostrils quivering, smells the wolf
whose white eye expands into a moon rising out of the trees,
and he trots in finally across the fields to the stable.
And the bats swim from their perches, the owls swoop;
and the frogs set up their din at the river.
And while the house fills with voices and footfalls
and laughter, and a fire crackles in the parlor, we sit
alone on the porch watching the ghost-play of the moths;
for though we embraced this day dreaming fire and measuring music,
we have gradually allowed the embracing darkness to hum us
         beyond ourselves,
to the acknowledgment—difficult for a visitor after all—
that the dance is come to us, that in the complexity of so much
bare horizon it is a congregation of dancers and singers
that simplifies things, reaffirming the simplicity
of men and women seasoned for birth and death each day of their lives,
sweetened by pain and aching with pleasure,
and, like the stars, best seen in constellations.

ATHENS, 1983

1. Omonia Square

A single bulb burns in a white room.
The table is covered with ikons.
A man is rinsing cherries in the sink.
Through the curtain, the blue H
of a hotel sign flutters.
The night swarms with sparks,
traffic ebbs and flows,
and the moon, with its winter light,
sweeps the streets menacingly—
but it is July, soft and steamy.
The man has come to the window now.
He's naked, wearing boots and sunglasses.
There is no one on the bed
to switch off the light.
There is no bed anymore.
It's a simpler room.
The table, the ikons, and the cherries
in a bowl of water.
By morning the water will be red.

2. Back Street

It is so dark, dark blue,
and the current that connects
night to morning has been severed.
Pedestrians and motorists will never
reach their destinations.
Even the motorcyclist, brazen
and abstracted, is doomed forever
to figure-eight his inclinations.
In the empty garage,
among tool racks and oil cans,
the pin-up girls stare out
from gauzy posters.
And in a doorway, a man
in white (policeman or pimp?)

beckons with authority;
where desire fails,
there is always subterfuge,
or—without a sound—
another murder.

3. Cats

Descended from Socrates' friends,
forty centuries of inbreeding
and they home in the ruins
of unfinished highrises—
construction-site lovers with the fast eyes.
Of the many thousands,
there is the occasional male calico,
and—rarely—the powerful loner,
emerged from the rabble
like the old dictators;
he's the one on the highest beam,
supine but dangerous,
gazing not down, but up—
knowing well that his subjects
will follow suit
yet never see beyond him.

MARS AND VENUS

Mars and Venus shine red and green
in the late-night sky,
odd flecks in the spilled milk
of the stars.
The wind strips the trees
from east to west
as we cross the river swiftly,
never sure where the shadows
leave off and the shore begins,
sure of nothing except
the other's presence
and the fish circling below,
the murky clockwork ballet
of their feeding.
If we were here to fish,
things would be simpler.
They would hasten to our lines
on such a night—its air
of cool density after the day's
unfocused heat—
and swallow the bright hooks
and flap up into the breathless
place, this other world,
and we could be certain
of their gratitude
for having helped them
enter eternity so singularly,
in flying arcs.
If, cutting the silk surface
in our light skiff,
we had only the pleasure of
Mars and Venus, ruby and emerald,
to distract us in this white &
black continuum of autumn nights,
there would be no reason
to distinguish the shadows

from the shore,
no purpose either in steering
to the one shore or the other,
in moving swiftly
or drifting with the ebb tide.
There would be only
the wind-stripped trees
and the fabulous sky
and the blackness,
riding the two of us,
you in green, I in red,
to its own destination,
with all those fish waiting,
like us, to be caught.

JEOFFRY THE CAT

The pale fields flow like the sea
in the darkening light.
Jeoffry keeps watch over me,
the two of us balanced
on the scales of the living God.
I drop to my knees
as the deadly moon alights
on the black hill
and the soft armies gather.
I see them there seeing me.
A man in London with a telescope
has cataloged my every sin.
Smart, Christopher. *Insanus.*
My heart is one star
he will never chart,
its lick of white flame blackening.
Jeoffry has seen the birds
of paradise in far galaxies,
the revolutions of dying suns,
the flickering angels in orchestra;
seen it all, unamazed,
in the fix of his jeweled eye.
I must not feed him meat or fowl.
Nor scraps of human prayer.
Nor slop of human desire.
Within these walls beating,
our two hearts merge
their singing chambers.
Our keeper, long-fallen
to his present state, gapes
at me and asks what I scribble
each dawn staring southward.
A song of that red meadow,
I whisper, where the blind girls
dance their ancient step.
A song no one will hear.

Only Jeoffry hears the bells
that ring dark and light
in the fast skies of creation.
Jeoffry who licked the Baptist's head
and curled round Jesus' foot
by the lepers' well.
I am a mad Englishman,
more hound than jaguar,
more highwayman than cleric,
more brokenhearted than they suspect.
I eats the leavings.
I writes the pauses.
I bathes with hard wine.
Jeoffry he crosses this cell
fused with holy intelligence
and airy health,
his forepaws lifted
to the burning air.
When I die they must let him
to the road, his mission,
to grace the original rhythm
of the ringing of dark and light,
the glass road that spirals
and may not end,
that I shall never see.

THE OTHER WOMAN

Pleasure alone can give us knowledge of things.
                              —GÉZA CZÁTH

One door opens, another closes.
Quick steps echo in the next street.
I recall with reverence
my moments of blind passion,
the sweet nights disordered,
music shaking the walls—
all in the name of salvation.
The holy war of the body and its pleasures.

The shadows of forgotten lovers
float down the unlit street,
their sea of darkness like gasoline—
waiting for the tossed match.
At the Protestant Cemetery in Rome,
gone to pay respects to the bones
of Keats, the heart of Shelley
(snatched from the fire),

a girl on each arm—
friends, sisters, opposite numbers . . .
What does it matter now?
The memory pays its dividends
with painful efficiency,
always in currency that cannot be spent.
One girl loved the moon over the white campagna.
The other was restless and eager to leave.

I chose between them, and I chose badly.
One door opens, another closes.
There is a clatter in the next street.
Once, at such a time, I lost something to the night.

Waiting for the Revolution

By way of the death of another
gunrunner on a slippery stairway
in the harbor of Montevideo,
of another femme fatale
in a basement in Tokyo,
we find our earnest endeavors
once again in vain.
Huddled in shabby rooms,
cooking stew in the can
and printing our manifestoes
in red and blue,
we ask ourselves what is at stake
if not a vision of the people
for the people to embrace.
What is politics, after all,
but the art of scurrying
in the pit, of men clawing
and slipping in a mire
of profound sin and ignorance.
Church and state agree on this.
And the revolution, before
it becomes the new state,
the better religion,
should be a sea of hands uplifted,
sweet with blood and ashes,
hands of iron that will have overturned
the corrupt and dusty diorama
of the chosen day
(henceforth, Independence Day)
in order to attempt the impossibility
of a clean slate:
the last manifesto suddenly
the new constitution,
the promised reforms codified,
and our surviving compatriots—
scribes and saboteurs,

gunrunners and femme fatales—
awarded their various commissions,
a crisp new flag run up
and all the rest of it;
the impossibility in the end
of attempting to impose
form, order, and goodwill
onto the great mass of men,
not to mention the handful
who believe their own promises.

It will never happen.

VOYAGE

Double and triple exposures of the shore
from a few miles at sea. Where the green
deepens to blue and the currents swell,
and the hills walling the continent blur away,
marking the beginning and end of our personal geography,
the soil that sprung us in a blinding rain.
The sun reflects back last night's moonlight,
a creamy mist in which gulls evaporate
and ambergris sizzles and sperm whales play out
their pantomime with harpoons: the ambivalent light
of purgatory, each of us with a few feet of railing
debating whether to leap or vomit or clutch for dear life.
We have been on many ships—which are as one.
Many seas—which are truly one.
To what point do we arc when our straight line falters?
For surely the passage to death is an extended curve—
like lovers who swoon through the many
small deaths of falling in and out of love,
giving up the ghost of the solitary spirit
each time the body makes its warmer connections.
With an umbrella to promenade the deck,
to orbit the little world of the ship each night
while others make the smaller orbit of the ballroom,
soft-shoeing themselves into situations,
we find that in a twinkling—
a handful of days and nights—
we are already far out to sea, between ports,
somewhere in the luscious indigo of our map,
and we feel not so much lost as found:
in position at last to encounter
the stray angels out of limbo, the freak dolphins
with wings, and the sea gods risen from drowned men;
in position, all tethers cut, to ascend dreaming
into the salt sky while Botticelli's girls play violins.
And if that doesn't work out (as it surely won't),
there is always our destination to fall back on;

from the crowded deck, the cold railing,
we can watch the blue swell taper to green,
gulls reappearing and cameras clicking:
double and triple exposures again, from a few miles out—
that same shore, come around the world for us
as if we had never left.

FILM NOIR

For Paul & Allison

The girl on the rooftop stares out
over the city and grips a cold revolver.
Laundry flaps around her in the hot night.
Each streetlight haloes a sinister act.
People are trapped in their beds, dreaming of
the A-bomb and hatching get-rich-quick schemes.
Pickpockets and grifters prowl the streets.
Hit-men stalk informers and crooked cops hide in churches.
Are there no more picket fences and tea parties
in America? Does no one have a birthday anymore?
Even the ballgames are fixed, and the quiz shows.
Airplanes full of widows circle the skyline.
Young couples elope in stolen cars.
All the prostitutes were wronged terribly in childhood.
They wear polka dot skirts, black gloves, and trenchcoats.
Men strut around in boxy suits, fedoras, and palm-tree ties.
They jam into nightclubs or brawl in hotel rooms
while saxophone music drowns out their cries.
The girl in the shadows drops the revolver
and pushes through the laundry to the edge of the roof.
Her eyes are glassy, her hair blows wild.
She looks down at her lover sprawled on the sidewalk
and she screams.
A crowd gathers in a pool of neon.
It starts to rain.

CROSSING PAROS AT DAWN

Grinding the silence like glass, we rode
our motorcycle to the crest of that hill
where the mules, in troikas, circled
the threshing floor under the farmer's whip,
and the valley of wild thyme flowed around
the monastery and the abandoned airstrip,
rippling clouds of scent over the vineyards,
up into the lemon groves.

Provisioned with bread and plums,
we bypassed the crossroads and stopped
at the village near the ravine
for coffee, and then at the marble quarry
where the wind howled out of the caves
trailing plumes of dust
and the sun burned watery shadows
around the chapel on the cliff.

Once over the river plain, we sped
into the forest and watched the sea
loom up through the pines,
its wall of mist curtaining off
Naxos' bluffs and blurring Ios
into a ghost ship on the northern horizon,
making us feel as if we ourselves were
riding the waves as we entered the mountains.

We climbed a long spiral,
kicking up clouds of gold and lapis
which anticipated us tier by tier—
rising to greet us—reminders of
the immediate past, just as the wide
vistas, dotted with Doric ruins and Crusaders'
castles, kept us attuned to the remote past,
its sweeps of color stilled into luminescence.

~

At the peak, the road leveled and widened
along the spine of the mountains;
limestone boulders walled off the sheer
drop, bats slept in the overhangs,
and orange lizards scrambled up
the rockface into crevices and fissures
as we roared around a succession
of hairpin turns, in and out and in . . .

Over this rutted stretch, locked in
that peculiar, quasi-lotus position,
our sunglasses dust-caked, and kidneys
shaken free of their sedentary poisons
(from that other life we had somehow escaped),
and the hardblue sky within easy reach,
we could let our minds wander
as coolly as light over stone.

Just as the old poets knew that true
vision—and purest delight—
materialized only when they peered inward,
so the traveler must pay close attention
to the intricate landscapes unfolding
behind the eye—not as reflections
but fiery constructions rushing across
the imagination's map in search of definition.

In sleep, in the airiness of a hotel
bed by a warm sea, with foreign voices
below, we're free to work some form
into the previous day's rambles, mingling
wonder, dread, and latent expectations
into the epoxy that will cement
our dreams—until they are dislodged
by other places, other sleep.

But as we crossed those mountains,
the tiger lilies dancing like flames
and pollen swirling into our eyes,
and the cicadas whirring mad harmonies,
this duality of landscape was not so obvious:

I could not close my eyes; the night lay
far away; and our journey through the interior
carried the insular resonance of too many dreams.

The birds at that altitude glided close
to the ground, oblivious to our intrusion—
Pissarro's quick strokes come to life,
hyphenating the hazy light,
darting across the rough plateau,
gathering in the trees, and spilling over
onto the next plateau like confetti—
canaries & thrush, bluejays & cardinals.

And all the while the sky softened
into greener tints, then yellows,
and the conversations of strangers and dead
acquaintances hummed in my ears in friendly—
even musical—tones, and you said you heard
someone following us, another motorcycle,
but when we stopped to look back,
there was no one—just the dust, and the birds.

And up high, barely visible, the half-moon
hung precariously from a pink cloud,
like those novelty items in store windows
that defy gravity (with magnets),
and if it didn't plunge seaward, I thought,
surely it would wafer into nothingness,
strayed from its nocturnal course, there
to shadow us all through the day, like the past.

Then suddenly we were descending:
the last glittering slope with its scrub-vines
and cactus, and the road curling down into
the salt-flats where miniature whirlwinds
might spin up at any moment, down and around
the marshes and over the scarred dunes,
to the sea that awaited us, the coral
reefs efflorescing red and green.

~

And far from shore an hour later,
our backs to the swell, the brine stinging,
we gazed in at the road threading
its limestone boulders like beads,
winding past the flowers and the forest
and the quarry, back to the port town,
the third-floor room on the harbor
where the sun had just blanketed our empty bed.

Elegy for E—

A woman holding her hat against the wind
crossed my shadow crossing 61st Street
the night your sister died.
But her dark coat, her scarf, barely stirred
even when the trees along the park
flapped in the gusts of the approaching storm.
It was a storm that never arrived,
like the children your sister never had,
the suitors her mother deflected,
the fruits of the earth that eluded her,
set in a bowl on the edge of a great cold table;
they ripened for death and death took them.
The table turned into a black sea
and a woman wearing a large hat sailed in on a skiff.
When she left, she took away the sky, the moon,
the trees—everything went over the horizon forever.
No angels sang. No one whispered any names.
The wind sent a single gray wave back to shore
and it never broke.

BLOOD TEST

LeRoy describes a dog, whose great-grandfather was a wolf, and this dog showed a trace of its wild parentage only in one way, by not coming in a straight line to his master when called.

—CHARLES DARWIN, The Origin of Species

I often wonder when they'll find the wolf in me.
The stray cell darkly circling the pack.
From the windows of northern cities
the same pale girl has beckoned me
many times over the years.
The one who climbed the tower
in a blizzard to watch the hammer-god
draw lightning from the midnight sun;
who buried jewelry under a cherry tree
and waited for the fruit, pitted
with rubies, to dot the spring snow;
who, in hotter climates, hid in my dreams
and woke me with her cold breath.

I look to the moon in Stockholm and Copenhagen,
that blazing zero in the polar sky,
to the stars whose needles of light
cannot penetrate my veins, nor pinpoint
the crook of despair in my bloodline;
instead, with my tropical compass,
my southern blood, they lure me into darkness.
We are all lured in the end,
by the ghost behind a window
or the burning wolf on a frozen lake,
to some doorway where the hot&cold
hands of death yank us from the shadows—
our own hands.

MOUNTAIN AND VALLEY

The full measure of all unknown quantities
resides in music, in the crumpled foil
of breaking waves and the bridges of passion
that connect the members of the string quintet.

Such music shivers a line of flame up
from the horizon, melting the darker clouds
onto the mountaintop, transfiguring them
into bodies at play, in limpid shadow.

Like perfect statuettes out of the past,
loved ones poised with toys and fruit of snow,
with forgotten conversations on their lips,
they wave to us from the top of the world.

Scattered as we are, here below,
projected by Mercator and divined by Aquinas,
we write music in our well-heated chambers,
we perform haltingly, or smoothly, but we cannot wave back.

We can be sure only of the future
advancing on us from the rear,
and the past (its godlike phantoms)
pulling us forward, into places that we dread.

A few madmen scale the mountain,
their ears lulled by the tapering winds,
their voices crackling into silence,
as they leave behind all burdens of health and weather.

But the rest of us remain in the valley,
in the clotted, musical air
where one day death, disguised as a peddler,
will arrive with a tonic, a solution,
a beautiful message from those people on the mountain.

Two Comedians

(after the painting by Edward Hopper)

His last canvas depicts two spry
white clowns (male & female)
taking a farewell bow on a vast stage,
spotlit before an echoing darkness.

The city droned with hornets that summer
and the birds fled his window two by two,
winding into the dusky sky.
Wielding brush like scalpel, he worked
his way through the bright shadows one last time.
After fifty years, here was the artist, here the model:
man and wife, lovers, clowns . . . like cats, or nightingales,
certain to die within a year of each other.
She grew old in the rooms he painted,
the motels and offices, automats and diners,
gazing out across miles of rooftops
into the blue American night.
She knew that when he laid down his brush
their bodies must follow,
spinning down into that clear, sad light
where everyone is always laughing.

III

RADIUM

The black lacquered urn etched with mountains
and glowing stars might best have displayed
camellias on a bedside table.
It holds the ashes of a T'ang prince
killed in an avalanche in his twenty-first year.
Excavated in a uranium mine, 2000 miles
from Peking, estranged from all imperial
relics of that or any other dynasty,
it was buried long enough for the pitchblende's
radium to fleck its luminosity
onto those stars alone.
Now the entire urn is radioactive,
with an astronomical half-life that prevents
meddling by human hands;
so we cannot be sure the prince's
ashes do not also glow—
that small measure of diamond dust
which one winter, as flesh and blood,
crossed the Empire, and on a mountain
crag at the frontier,
upon hearing a rumble above,
murmured his amazement to a silent retainer,
his words glinting for an instant
in the rush of snow.

BLUE CURRENTS

... perhaps the resurrection of the soul after death is to be conceived as a phenomenon of memory.

—MARCEL PROUST, *Le Côté de Guermantes*

After another dark interlude
the voice in the night returns us to the hill
where the meteors shower in white and gold,
where solitary under the dizzying pines
we recall our deeper obligations to ourselves,
the colors that highlight our inner spaces—
the intricate seismology of our oceans and plains.
Those pines hooked the streaking stars and hung them
at their peaks like the ornaments of rare dreams.
And the white road spiraling up that hill,
dusty and moonlighted as memory itself,
winds over stone bridges and streams,
past fields strewn with childhood debris,
toys and trinkets and the bright links of days
snapped from the chain of events that led us here.
We may as well calculate the distance between Neptune
and Saturn in human miles, intending to cover it on foot,
as attempt to chart the galaxies of our hearts and minds
with the base instruments of science.
It is reassuring to believe we are different
from preceding generations, whose works we sleep upon,
whose breath and bodies (if Lucretius is to be trusted)
now constitute our rainfall, dust, and fire.
We would like to think ourselves the first men,
and perhaps secretly we hope to be the last.

But lying on the dark hill, diving into black seas
behind our closed eyes, what is it we hope to salvage
in those currents we can no longer see or feel?
What wrecks lie honeycombed with the gold of our unlived
days, the treasure of the future barnacled and surrounded
by the patrolling sharks and electric eels of our past?
Salvation hovers beyond those wrecks
and we are permitted one chance at it

(just as this is the only road to the hilltop and its meteors),
one entry unique, seasonal, and ever-shifting,
through blue currents that, once navigated, forever
carry us safely, and deeply, where we most feared to go.

There is a certain way of seeing the world.
The people, and the many places.
You go from A to B to C
and you keep your eyes open,
especially in the dark.
Stay on your toes and off the ropes.
Hone your wits on fear.
Don't talk about nightmares,
the queerer things.
No one ever really knows enough
to say enough to help
illuminate the walls
on your blind side;
indeed, every man has one eye sharper
than the other,
sharper even than his heart.
As for the big ideas,
Love & the rest,
take the simplest straight sentence
and move on from there.
Better the one clean dive
(however short)
than a lifetime of twists and turns.
The world is so full of good things
and interesting evil things
and the truly interesting in between
that you must never let up.
But don't tell people too much
or they'll spoil it for you.
They won't take to the notion
that the wider passion,
the sweetest moments,
can never be duplicated
but only grafted delicately
against all odds
in the cold climate

of the finest art.
You avoid the private hell
with the more private pleasures.
For years and years
diminishing yourself
day by day.
You ask yourself when it all began,
when it ended,
whose words were borrowed for the journey,
and why, with luck, they sometimes worked.
Then, when the light dims,
you kill it.

NIGHT OF THE QUARTER-MOON IN AUGUST

The cherry blossoms swirl
around the brightening rim,
up over the point and down
the concave slide and around again:
blood- and milk-flecked scythe
in the snow-white sky.

The tension of mountains looming
and black field streaming
away from us, throwing sparks,
provides the first tingling intimation
of bad sleep:
bedlam behind a lit screen.

Postcard oddities displace our memories:
Arctic and Aegean dawns overlaid;
weeping underwater palms;
tinted landscapes and awkward nudes:
these will take us only so far,
and then combust.

Left stranded with starry sky—
like the black cat on the white roof,
the astronomer spiraling into vertigo—
we look down and away, over pines,
into meadows, along stark roads,
searching out what the lightning grounds.

We sense somewhere this night a friend
is failing, blood-novas in the brain,
clot dispatched from artery to lung,
failing, the mute ache and fury of the body
washed over with death before the living eye,
failing—as the moon fails, its blade of light.

POSTCARD FROM ALBANIA
For David

Let's face it, comrade, the land
of milk and honey is here and now
under the sign of Cancer.
Love is flowing through razor-sharp
rapids, powering ancient turbines,
so the lights of Tirana
will twinkle under a red sky.

This is a Moslem country without mosques.
Across the strait lies gay Italy,
to the south sunny Greece.
"Wanted" posters of King Zog
(exiled in Spain) hang near
the statues of Stalin and Mao,
and the newspapers predict
a Russo-American invasion—tomorrow.
All the taps run icewater.
The hotel doors don't lock.

At night the wind carries ashes
down from the mountains, indigo
snow-peaks shooting off strange fires—
like the lighting in a black comedy
that makes the demons look funny
when you're least expecting it.
Was Marlowe right—is Ignorance the only evil?
There are tortures we know nothing about,
from which the torturers, too,
derive pain, and smile.

The House Where Lord Rochester Died

The embarrassment of the swans
in the bedroom mural fleeing
the milkmaids in the satyr's bath;

and the storm clouds—rendered
so delicately by well-paid hands—
creeping westward, trailing the orgy;

and the orchids still moist
and flush in the cherub's mouth . . .
In this mural, as out the bay window,

the prospect of rain appears endless,
the hayfield swirls with pollen—
the vistas merge across time.

This confusion of nature and art,
overlapping so casually,
leaves us dizzy as we back out of the room,

through the padded doors and down
the icy stairwell, across a gallery
of spidery light where we find,

fired in dust on a bare wall,
the imprint of a man
shielding his eyes, wiping his mouth.

THE CARNIVAL AT MIDNIGHT

... making our dull rounds
of the Carnival, after hours,
under a black tinfoil sky,
garish posters dusted silver
and moonlight slanting in
at a deathly angle,
we wonder if that was a footfall
in the shadows—
a malingering spectator
or just another prowler
from the train yards
hungry for a peek
at the lady acrobats
and a free meal
outside the strongman's tent.
In this rutted lot,
once a wheatfield,
men swallow fire and swords,
dive into washtubs
from great heights,
and gnash titanium like toast.
But now they're sleeping
or playing cards,
and across the blond wastes of America,
beyond the Rocky Mountains
and the last fiery waterfall,
someone from our distant past
is dreaming us as we are,
in nightwatchman's black,
threading our way
between tents and trailers,
hat in hand, dusty,
with a lump in the throat that—
like a thousand-to-one shot—
may pay off
in still another poem

or rich romance.
Our dreamer knows
we harbor too much
of the Byron we read
in early youth
on summer nights,
and still expect gypsy girls
with flashing bracelets
to prance through beaded curtains
while ouds wail
and houris clap.
Instead, the guard-dogs bay
on the factory grounds,
and the interstate hums
with demented insistence,
and our sweetheart,
from the wrong side
of the tracks,
comes to us with a new complaint
and a cold embrace.
Nothing falls right
in these shadowy times.
Like sprung clocks
or fizzled bulbs,
we appear helplessly intact—
only our insides gone wrong.
In the highest windows
of platinum cities
we cast smart silhouettes
gazing out over
the moist landscape
of fluency and success,
the webwork of colored lights—
but that was a different
lifetime, another kind of night.
Here, where the jugglers reign
supreme, and the vanishing act
(twin girls in trick-closets) never fails,
and the bearded lady sings
like a canary in her bath,
there is no godlike perspective

from on high, no Olympic bemusement—
men and women lord it over
their momentary reality,
turning the tables on Newton
and Galileo, amazing the children
with their dog-eared feats.
But the children gone
and the floodlights doused,
gravity weighs them down again
with the best of us.
Sleep refrigerates their fine talents.
So many of them drinkers, brawlers,
and insomniacs,
and we—doubly, trebly—intruders
in their midst, even now
with the great show packed away,
come to observe, to take,
and to relinquish nothing
but our anxious fears.
When finally we have left
the Carnival behind,
moving with haste,
with no backward glance,
until some miles north,
when the moon has dipped
behind the hills,
we pause long enough to survey
the blinking lamps
in the torn-up field,
the patched tents and ghostly trailers,
to hear one last lion's yawn
across the humid flats,
and to spot the single human form,
sexless, compact, tiny,
crossing the highwire
in the open air,
arms outstretched, head erect—
an acrobat sleepwalking?
Or that prowler,
still looking for something,
his eyes trained on distant planets.

BLONDES AND BRUNETTES

Combing the countryside for them.
The cities and islands, the open road.

That wilderness of American women,
waiting for conquistadors and saints—

or is it the men who are waiting
to be conquered and sanctified?

At one&twenty I never waited:
I chased and courted,

offering whatever I had at hand—
poems, lilacs, ocean dreams . . .

It's all a blur now.
Sweet as lemon blossoms and mist,

as the mountain rains back then
that washed me free of myself.

Sweet as the euphony of the heart
that lulled me through storms,

and the clouds of swallows
out my window at dawn,

and the exhausting seduction
refrains in the packed night.

That life, with its golden fires,
took my breath away one time too many.

Just as dark eyes and darker voices
lighted the road away from death.

CONSTRUCTION SITE, WINDY NIGHT

Great plastic sheets are flapping
twenty stories up, east and south,
where tinted windows will look out
over the park next summer,

and widows will draw their blinds,
and men gripping iced drinks talk
about money and death
while the moon slides between clouds;

and up another ten stories,
the foreman's corrugated shack
rattles, and the rats tip
a pail of rivets onto the floor

where cats will doze, and young
girls waltz, and lovers groan,
oblivious of wild parties above
and children howling below;

and even higher, on the roof,
a flock of pigeons lines the railing,
and they will remain as they are,
scanning the blotted trees

and mating and sleeping
and squinting at the odd visitor
who will venture up on a summer night
to be alone or to meet someone,

to escape an argument
or to connect with the cosmos,
to stare down from that windy perch
at his fellow-citizens

~

crossing streets and hailing cabs
and think how far away they are,
and how the things men construct
in their minds can materialize

suddenly, towering over them
and filling them with dread of heights.

Icarus

The rumbling sky splinters with light.
Girls are dancing on the silver yacht,
blaring music out to sea.
After another drinking bout, the architect's
son wants to show them his new toy.
He climbs to the crow's nest, straps on
some wings, and leaps for the sun:
the boiling waves swallow him with a hiss.
The girls keep on dancing
and the shoreline blackens with rain.
After the funeral, in a foreign capital,
the architect designs an obelisk for his son's grave.
The priests tell him that all men die happy.
That night he dreams himself lost
in the labyrinth that made him famous,
pursued down the iron corridors
by sparking hoofs, through smoke
reeking of perfume and blood,
into a fiery tunnel . . .
He wakes in a cold sweat, clutching a ball of string.
Maybe the priests were right.
Or maybe in the end fools like his son
chance on a kind of wisdom, coveting a final
futile gesture in order to cheat death.
One could do worse, he concludes,
drawing the taut sheet to his chin,
like a knife, and closing his eyes
on a pair of beating wings.

VERONA, 1973

Or to the anonymous woman
on the steps of the church
who casts no shadow,
to her passive, frozen silence,
I offer the relief
of my distracted motions
crossing the square to
the shuttered house where
I hope to make a conquest
over tea and violins.
I inhale the clouds of scent
from the flowerbeds
and count the poplars hazed
in that perpetual past—
the summer's day—
that backpedaling
with one eye unfocused,
intense with heat,
impatient as the girl alone
in bed with the kicked-
off sheets, the coldwater
spill by her pillow.

In the vestry, in shadow,
the priest who will confess
that solitary woman
caresses the butcher's boy,
dying of cancer;
overhead, a single shaft
of light lemons the sifting dust,
the lonely circle of brick,
but leaves the real darkness
untouched, pouring down.

BLIZZARD

White on white, the River
Nile, the Yangtze—
I'm dreaming of rivers
while the heavy snow
blows into the city night,
blanking the streetlamps
and sliding across my window
rough as sand.
The purple banks of the Ganges
catch no snow,
though the crocodiles'
throats are lined with ice,
their icicle teeth glint,
and their eyes, candle-
lit, glow like moons
in a winter sky.
Over the prairies
the black snow advances
in white sheets,
buries fences, dissolves trees,
a thousand prairies coast to
coast drifting into
a single shade of white.
Fanning out into the jungle,
the Amazon shimmers
under the wings of golden birds,
and over these rooftops
the flying snow
obscures chimneys and water towers,
bridges and smoke,
it camouflages cars
and paves the street for angels
until finally all the rivers
in the world stop flowing
and I reach the end
of my dream riding a waterfall

that never ends,
and on my roof
two thick feet of snow
to reflect the morning sun.

Orange Light

A slice of orange light crosses
the cat's tail on the windowsill.

Messengers from beyond the grave send
their reassurances on this sultry afternoon.

They arrive in the form of singing telegrams,
fluttering down from the high-voltage wires.

No one can say how this is done.
The cat, dreaming of cats, doesn't care.

He once belonged to the stranger upstairs.
Then the stranger disappeared.

The mirrors in strangers' rooms open onto
other rooms and tell us nothing about death.

Their dead speak to one another
in those rooms in hushed cadences.

Out the window, orioles build palatial nests
and white spiders hieroglyph the fruit.

The orange tree leans into the hard wind.
Beyond it, the two lakes ripple, one after the other.

We are dreaming again
that this summer passed us by long ago,

that these same birds have flown for centuries
and only we have come and gone, clamoring,

bringing the world out of oblivion with us
and then taking it back again, too soon.

The cat glances into the mirror. The light palls.
Everyone dies sending messages, trying to fly.

Notes at Summer's End

All night, the long night of cars inching
westward on glowing highways, radios tuned
to the Prophet Elijah of Trenton delivering his
"celestial weather report" in a fretful monotone,
droning on about floods, eagles, and salvation

while I lie awake into the morning listening
to a different message out of the prickly darkness
that canopies my street and shields my neighbors
from the cold business of the stars, the lives
and deaths of comets, the moon's ebb and flow.

All night while the babies nestle into vaporous
sleep, and the girls from the heartland toss
homesick in furnished rooms, and the old men stare
through the slats of their insomnia, I wait
in my own niche on the continent's edge for sunrise

the way some men wait all their lives for
the right woman or a pile of money or a chance
at redemption, for that sweet lottery ticket
of the spirit which will free them finally
from anguish, heartbreak, and lurking shadows.

All night there have been strange lights to
the north, golden haloes in the south—so many
false intimations of sunrise that one might conclude
our earth has gone astray, sailing into the sun,
or away from it, to some grim suburb of the cosmos.

And after I have convinced myself the dawn
has failed me, messengers—wingéd like
white birds you have never seen, their hair
streaming out behind them green and blue—
come to me with bursting hearts and sing,

~

all night a hundred, a thousand choruses encircle
me singing in unison of the hour of reawakening,
of brilliant revelation, of all the things
we are told to pray for but never to expect,
and I listen like a true believer,

like my compatriots out in the rain in their
dark cars, with only the voice of the Prophet
Elijah to keep them company, hammering
their loneliness into submission, and their own
faces, limned on glass, staring back at them,

all night so alone, apart from all of these,
the babies and the farmgirls and the geriatrics,
I feel more connected to them than ever
because I am afraid, and my fear has charged me,
because like the heavens that have burst

open for me on bright blinding hinges,
the hearts of the millions of strangers with whom
I share this planet and its oblivion have opened
as well, all at once, like a silent furnace,
ignorant of its many parts but not of its whole,

all night burning with unbearable heat
until the dawn, when even in summer,
even when I am not alone or vigilant,
even when the midnight sweats a tropic-black,
the sea wind must blow in cold, to cool me.